ON THE
OTHER SIDE

S.E. McKenzie

S. E. MCKENZIE

ISBN- 1928069290

ON THE OTHER SIDE

DEDICATION

To everyone who has been left out in the cold.

S. E. MCKENZIE

This book is a book of speculative fiction. Characters, companies, governments, places, events, are either products of the author's imagination or used fictitiously. Any resemblance to persons (living or dead), companies, governments, places and/or events, is a coincidence.

ON THE OTHER SIDE

TABLE OF CONTENTS

ON THE OTHER SIDE

ON THE OTHER SIDE

I

Once I was asleep in my bed
I slept through the night
Only to be awoken by an awful fright

The ground shook
And something roared
Underneath me

So drowsy was I
I didn't ask why
The rumble didn't crumble

The earth beneath my bed.
I was jolted from peaceful slumber
How could I do more than only grumble?

Now as I reflect,
I still don't understand
The power of such force

S. E. MCKENZIE

Was it the invisible hand?
So living
And unforgiving

Possibly the invisible hand was not living
Beneath my floor?
Possibly this unknown force was death

A body without hope or breath
Possibly a spirit floating by
Who couldn't reach the sky

But why was such force stirring under my bed
Why wasn't it
Stirring somewhere else instead?

Then I remembered his name
A man whose last years brought such great sorrow
Yes, such force could be stirring from Billy Joe

ON THE OTHER SIDE

From days gone by
This man was certain
To not have reached the sky

And as I lost myself in thought
I just assumed
Billy Joe had turned to rot

The roar it grew
And the floor did shake
I was sure it must be his rage

Causing this earthquake
For his rage
Brought gloom and doom

Even though
His guilt was always denied
I always thought that Billy Joe had lied

He always begged to be heard
Even though
The world turned its back on him

S. E. MCKENZIE

That is how I remember Billy Joe
Though he always claimed his innocence
There was never a doubt

In most people's minds
It was Billy Joe to blame
For the deed that caused Mary Jane to die in pain

And that is why Billy Joe
Had not just been a prisoner in a cage
He had also been imprisoned by his rage

Until the day he died

Yes, his rage could have been stirring
So alone without peace
Still shackled and buried

Some place under the ground
In the abyss
Covered with morning mist

A legend from years gone by
Who couldn't reach the sky
For it is said he could not let Mary Jane go

ON THE OTHER SIDE

To love another
So he took her life
With a butcher knife

A free spirit he could never possess
And how could his love be true
If he wouldn't let Mary Jane go

So she could be loved by another

II

Dead matter resting in eternity
Must be stirring, possibly
Hot mass deep in the ground

Made the ground around me rumble
I was sure the ground under my bed
Was about to crumble

There was nothing I could do
But only grumble
Hoping all would be well

Even though the roaring
Sounded like it was
Coming from Hell

S. E. MCKENZIE

III

And many would agree
And say free spirits
Can only enter heaven's gate

When they grow hearts free from hate

And others just can't understand
The tyrant spirit of persecution
For these men trying to gain social merit

Had no solution
As ancient spirits sought a home nearby
For they could not reach the sky

So they must join the chaos in the abyss below
For it had a greater pull
Than we will ever know

For the Earth's core; partly iron

Could warm the coldest heart
Even the heart of Billy Joe
For it was said

ON THE OTHER SIDE

That he would rather kill his true love
Than let her be possessed by another
So he was trapped for ever

In his grave below

In the abyss, to never be free
For Eternity
For he would never reach the sky

IV
Beyond this civilization
It was said
Chaos ruled in the abyss

V
And some would disagree
And would sell you
Hope of order for a fee

Others would persecute
Harass and oppress
And then send the bill

S. E. MCKENZIE

To the critical mass
Don't ask why
And don't you cry

Just confess and self-incriminate
So you can fit into the mold
Which feeds all this hate

Until you grow old they will let you eat
Let those who persecute force you to kneel
Decide your fate without standing on your feet

VI
And there is no way out
And that is why
Some die

Before they ever lived
Some begin to live
When they know they are going to die

ON THE OTHER SIDE

VII

Being awoken from my dream
I cursed this rage that roared
In the middle of the night

It just was not right
That a power from beneath
Had released its energy

Just to awake me
From my slumber
And I could only grumble

As I heard roars
In waves so loudly
Who else would have been turned to dust

And still exist so proudly?

S. E. MCKENZIE

VIII

If there was a way out
Of this hell hole
Billy Joe would find it

Yes I know

The force below the ground
Already knew
How to select and how to protect

And who to neglect

Gold, precious metals and gems
The need for them condemns
A fool to hard toil

Deep under the earth's soil

IX

Caught in the battle
Was never wise
For wounds would leave scars

ON THE OTHER SIDE

That will be despised
Leaving you open
To being criticized

Scars on the mind and in the heart
Will leave you shattered
And torn apart

Just like Billy Joe
Who died in a cage
Engulfed in rage

Billy Joe would always deny
That he was the one who took the life
Of his true love Mary Jane

With a butcher knife

X
Where does this abyss end?
Is it is in space
Where light is able to bend

Or does it end
Beneath our feet miles below
Or is it in the heart when it learns to mend

When one tries to possess love
It will over flow
Just ask Billy Joe

XI
For it was said
Billy Joe would rather kill
Than let his only love be with another

XII
The treasures beneath
Had been taken
Many years ago

And in their place
Emptiness was left
Surrounded by moving plates

And artificial snow

And this was the time
The ground would open
Revealing the curse that would spread

Even in the space below my bed

ON THE OTHER SIDE

A sinkhole hundreds of feet deep
Opened while my neighbor was still asleep
As he sunk into the earth

I was glad it was not me

XIII

The persecutor took what he could
And would have taken more
Until a judge came from the sky

And stopped the revolving door
With one mighty roar
That the wise could not ignore

XIV

I had a long way to go
After a hard day of work
Associating with those only

Pretending to be relating
Once I reached my destination
There would be a meal waiting

S. E. MCKENZIE

Once I arrived
I could put up my feet
Have something to eat

Always thankful that
I had survived
A hard day working nine to five

What else could I ask for
But an inside lock to my door
And to be safe

From polarization
And thoughtless chatter
So I could think about things

That really matter

XV
There were eyes everywhere

Watching those
In public space
Less privacy everyday

ON THE OTHER SIDE

As freedom faded away
The force became less understanding
And more demanding

As the tides
Fall and rise
Private eyes see through the disguise

While stony barriers shape public space
The homeless
Had no status or no space

To call their own

Or so he said
When he saw them asleep in the study hall
He could only see red

As they were made to feel so small

No rights as housing costs soar
Lost rights as the force
In the abyss could only roar

S. E. MCKENZIE

Citizenship
Refuge
From hardship

XVI

As he wore a crown
Never his own
He had the power to put them down

In a world growing meaner
Everyday
The bill was sent

To the mass so critical
Who were beginning to feel
Hopelessly cynical

When books and things
Had more rights
Than you and I

ON THE OTHER SIDE

We hoped for a dead man
To come from the sky
And to walk about and to ask why

We were waiting for a king
Who had no crown
We were waiting for something better

That wouldn't keep us down

So that we could live freely in harmony
And to entrust each other
With our humanity

XVII
They had no say
And no right to speak out loud
That is why they were lost in the crowd

XVIII
This is the other side
Now you have nowhere to hide
Now you will get kicked down

S. E. MCKENZIE

As you try to get up
You had your cup
With coins that were thrown in

Not much there
Just tokens from people
Who tried to share

In a land that grew colder everyday
The bulldozers tore down
All the shacks in the slum

The mood between the elite
And everyone else was very glum
Only saved by their show of compassion

Even though only a show
Hid hypocrisy and deception
For it was the fashion

To despise what the eyes saw

ON THE OTHER SIDE

XIX

People without disguise
Sleeping in the study hall
Was now against the law

When the homeless awoke
They felt so small
For they had no were to go

Where they could call their own
And were so alone
And lost in the crowd

XX

There were fishes from the sea
And loaves of bread
To share

Even though loitering in public space
Could open one to persecution
The man in the white robe

Sat on the hill with the solution
He began to explain,
"Your pain is my pain.

S. E. MCKENZIE

It will take a lot of love to learn to trust again,
In love we have so much to gain."
Then he saw the weapons

Of mass destruction
And he felt rage.
"Turn these weapons into plowshares

While you still can
Believe in the rights of man
For that is the only way

To grow Goodwill."

As the crowd grew
The man on the hill
Divided the food and made it multiply

Many were too hungry to wonder
How this was done
They only ate before they were forced to run

For other men were arriving
Each carrying a gun
Then they arrested the son.

ON THE OTHER SIDE

Everyone cried
It was a painful sight
The good was lost

That was the cost
The whistle it blew
So what could they do?

For this was life on the other side

XXI
They took the man
And made him stand by a tree
They told him that he was going against policy.

"We are just doing our job
Controlling the mob
They know it is against the law

To loiter or sleep in the study hall
We don't care where they go
As long as they stay

On the other side
That is the way
Of today."

Then another man came out of the grocery store
And started to complain.
"You there giving away food

What world do you think we are living in?"
"I know," said the man in white,
"This is the world of sin."

XXII
And where to begin
And when to end
In this world

You had to learn to bend
You had to turn away
While your heart

Tried to mend
For this was not
The way it should have been

ON THE OTHER SIDE

For it was true
And we all knew
This was paradise lost

That was the price
For the overkill
Of the underfed

XXIII

Fear of domination by foreigners
Made us trust the invisible hand more
As we all stood in polarized corners

We could not forget what had been lost
Made many of us mourners
While looking down upon others

Was not so easy now
As the man in white
Was still sitting by the tree

We were no longer allowed to rest in public places
For we were no longer free
Without freedom there was no privacy

S. E. MCKENZIE

The barriers blocked the way
So they could ghettoize
Many were too afraid to criticize

Many said these were the end days
As their negativity grew
So did their frown

But the man in white disagreed
And explained his point of view
He said evil would always try to deceive

But if we work together
There will be so much
We will be able to achieve

And love will make us strong
That is what we have to believe
Paradise is only lost

For it is buried
In all this conflict and tension
Beware of men of pretension

ON THE OTHER SIDE

For they will be wearing crowns and jewels
Beware of these men, for they are fools
I am here to show you a new direction

Only way to stop this war
Is to learn to love each other more
While the tyranny of evil

Is all around

XXIV

We all need
Someone to feed
Dying in all this greed

And we all knew that was true
We just did not know what to do
For other men arrived, and each had a gun

S. E. MCKENZIE

Many of us started to run
As the man in white sitting by the tree
Stood up and said

The deed you do this day
Will never fade away
For it will echo into eternity

XXV

The persecutor took what he could
And would have taken more
Until a judge came from the sky

And stopped the revolving door
And we never asked why
For we all knew

The dangers on Earth
Could spread
To the rest of the galaxy

ON THE OTHER SIDE

And the new world order
Was almost the same
It just had a different name

For it would take a lot of love
To work together and to unite
It would take a miracle

To turn this all around
And make it right
This is what we must do

We must open our arms
And welcome humanity
So we can try to prevent

World War Three.

THE END

S. E. MCKENZIE

ON THE OTHER SIDE
Produced by S. E. McKenzie Productions
First Print Edition January 2015

ISBN: 978-1-928069-29-4
Copyright © 2015 by S. E. McKenzie
All rights reserved.

Enquiries: 1(778)992-2453
Mailing Address:
S. E. McKenzie Productions
168 B 5th St.
Courtenay, BC
V9N 1J4

Email Address:
messidartha@aol.com

http://www.amazon.com/SarahMcKenzie/e/B00H9RWX48/ref=ntt_dp_epwbk_0